SALT & PEPPER
AT THE
PIKE PLACE MARKET

Written by Carol A. Losi

Illustrated by Amy Meissner

WESTWINDS PRESS®

Billy pulled the leash. "C'mon, boy," he said. "Let's go get our mussels." Pepper was confused. Where was Miss Lee? But Pepper was good at obeying.

Salt was not so good at obeying, but then Miss Lee commanded, "HEEL!" Salt was so surprised that he followed her. "Good girl," said Miss Lee.

At Sosio's Produce, Miss Lee said, "Ah, here are the vegetables. Sit, girl." Salt scratched his ear.

"What has gotten into you?" Miss Lee said, raising an eyebrow. "I said SIT!" Salt sat.

"That's better," said Miss Lee. "Here's an oyster mushroom for a treat." Salt gobbled it down.

Salt and Pepper had nothing in common, except, of course, that they looked exactly alike.

Salt was a sailor. He lived with Billy Bigelow and his father on a houseboat. Pepper was a princess. She lived in a penthouse apartment with Miss Mingyong Lee.

Salt loved seafood. Pepper did not.

Pepper was the star of her obedience school. Salt was not.

Salt and Pepper had nothing in common, *until* one morning in August, when they both went shopping at Seattle's Pike Place Market.

Let's buy some treats, boy. How about smoked mussels?" Billy asked Salt, pulling him through the crowd.

Salt barked. He loved smoked mussels.

"First stop: vegetables," said Miss Lee. "We're having tempura tonight. Stay close, Pepper. I don't want to lose you in this crowd."

It happened in front of the fish market. Suddenly, a fish flew, the crowd jumped, two leashes dropped, and . . .

Billy bought a bag of smoked mussels.

"Where should we go next?" he asked as they started down the stairs. He looked at Pepper and paused. "Hey boy. When did you learn how to heel?" He tossed Pepper a smoked mussel. "Good boy!"

Pepper was so surprised, the treat bounced off her nose.

On the second level, Salt barked and jumped at the window of the Giant Shoe Museum. The thought of chewing up those shoes always made him happy.

Miss Lee tugged at his leash.

"Stop that," she scolded.

Salt followed glumly. This was no fun.

At the Pike Place Magic Shop, Reuben the Magician made a ball appear in Billy's hand. The crowd cheered. When Reuben tried to make a ball appear under Pepper's paw, she barked at him and it didn't work. Pepper didn't like people tricks.

"That's okay, boy! Maybe next time," said Billy.

Got Magic?

WACKY NOSES

As he followed Miss Lee to the end of the hall, Salt smelled something familiar: smoked mussels?

As she followed Billy downstairs, Pepper thought she heard something familiar: high-heeled shoes?

On the last level of shops, Billy ran to the fortune-teller outside Old Friends Antiques and Collectibles. "Let's get our fortunes told," he said.

Billy's fortune read: "Make new friends, but keep the old." But Pepper didn't want a fortune. She just wanted to get away from the funny-looking fortune-teller.

When Miss Lee and Salt reached the last level, they stopped at Grandma's Attic.

"You look darling!" said Miss Lee.

Salt scratched and pulled at the lace. The doll clothes made him itch.

What's wrong now, girl?" asked Miss Lee. "The stairs are this way. Don't you want to go home?"

Home? Home was with Billy!

"Time to go," said Billy, pulling Pepper toward the ramp. "You can have a swim in the lake and eat the rest of the mussels when we get home."

But Pepper did not want to swim in lakes, and she never wanted to smell another stinky smoked mussel.

L̲et's pet the pig," said Billy, "and then we'll leave."

"Let's put some money in the pig," said Miss Lee, "for good luck."

Then it happened . . .

Miss Lee called, "Here, Pepper!"

Billy called, "Here, Salt!"

"Wow," said Billy, shaking his head. "That dog looks just like you."

"Good thing I know you so well," laughed Miss Lee, "or I might have taken home the wrong dog."

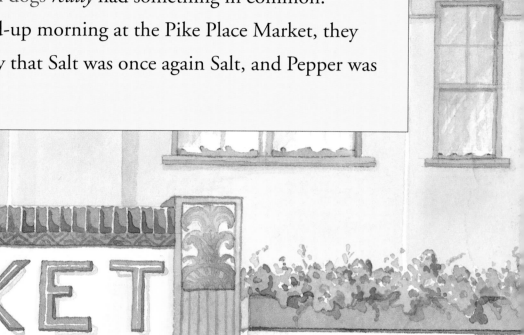

Now the twin dogs *really* had something in common.

After a mixed-up morning at the Pike Place Market, they were both happy that Salt was once again Salt, and Pepper was still Pepper.

For Mark, with whom I have everything in common.
And for Christy Silvas, who babysat.
—C. A. L.
For the good folks at the Pike Place Market—
thanks for making it all happen, every day.
—A. C. M.

Library of Congress Cataloging-in-Publication Data
Losi, Carol A.
    Salt and Pepper at the Pike Place Market / by Carol Losi ;
illustrated by Amy Meissner.
        p. cm.
    Summary: Two dogs that look identical, one who lives on a
    boat and one who is pampered in a penthouse apartment, get
    switched accidentally in Seattle's Pike Place Market.
        ISBN 1-55868-800-5 (hb) — ISBN 1-55868-801-3 (sb)
    1. Dogs—Juvenile fiction. [1. Dogs—Fiction.
    2. Mistaken identity—Fiction. 3. Markets—Fiction.
    4. Seattle (Wash.)—Fiction.] I. Meissner, Amy, ill.
    II. Title.
        PZ10.3.L89Sal 2004
        [E]—dc22   2004004087

Second printing 2005

WestWinds Press®
An imprint of Graphic Arts Center Publishing Co.
P.O. Box 10306, Portland, Oregon 97296-0306
503-226-2402 / www.gacpc.com

President: Charles M. Hopkins
Associate Publisher: Douglas A. Pfeiffer
Editorial Staff: Timothy W. Frew, Tricia Brown,
Jean Andrews, Kathy Howard, Jean Bond-Slaughter
Production Staff: Richard L. Owsiany, Susan Dupere
Editor: Michelle McCann
Designer: Andrea Boven Nelson, Boven Design Studio, Inc.

Printed in the United States of America

PIKE
PLACE
MARKET